BAND BOUND

From Blues to Success

Jane Beals

PINNACLE PRESS

From Blues to Success is the fifth in a five book series.
Brendon called the other three to him and said, "Okay!
Now remember what we've been practising. Let's not
let all that hard work go to waste. Let's give it everything
we've got."

Band Bound Series:

1   Before the Band

2   Becoming a Band

3   Born to Rock

4   Rock Band Blues

5   From Blues to Success

Band Bound – From Blues to Success
ISBN 9781906373078
Ordering Code – UK7001

Curriculum Concepts UK
The Old School
Upper High Street
Bedlinog
Mid-Glamorgan CF46 6SA
Email: orders@curriculumconcepts.co.uk
www.curriculumconcepts.co.uk

Copyright © Jane Beals 1995
First published in United Kingdom, 2007
Published by Pinnacle Press, NZ

Illustrated by Michelle Cooper

From Blues
to Success

Introduction

The Story So Far . . .

New Thyme, the band that Brendon, Gavin, Estelle and Libby formed after the school Talent Quest, had played well at the school dance and their friends really enjoyed it.

After taking on Martyn, a friend of Gavin's, as their manager, they played at a beach charity concert.

The band did not feel that they played well to suit the change in place and audience.

Libby was so upset that she quit the band and Brendon couldn't talk her into coming back.

The others decided to keep practising and to work at the things they weren't good at.

Chapter 1

The band had decided to have some extra practices to work on the things they weren't good at.

Martyn and Gavin suggested that they invite Ms Campbell along to listen.

"What for?"
asked Estelle.

"She knows a lot about music.
She knows about tone and balance,
from taking the orchestra,"
explained Gavin.

"Yeah, but an orchestra's a bit
different to a band,"
said Brendon.

"Not really, Brendon,"
said Martyn.
"The instruments are different,
but the ways to get good sound are
much the same."

"When I play in the orchestra,
I'm listening to how my part sounds
and how it fits into the whole sound.
I do the same in the band,"
explained Gavin.

"I guess so,"
agreed Brendon.

"Yeah, you've had more
experience than us,"
nodded Estelle.
"It's worth a try."

"She might not want to help,"
said Brendon.
"She's very busy."

Gavin blushed.

"Well I told her about the beach concert
the other day and the problems we
had.
She said she'd like to help if
we wanted."

"Great!
Can you ask her for Thursday?"
asked Estelle.

After agreeing to ask Ms Campbell
to come and listen to them play they
got onto the problem of Libby.

At their last practice the others
had suggested Gavin should talk
to her.

He had, but she'd kept saying that she wasn't coming back.

He felt that she really wanted to, but her stubborn nature wouldn't let her give in.

"I'll ring her again tonight,"
said Gavin. He thought it was worth having one more try.

"That would help, Gav.
She's been really unhappy all week.
I think you're right.
She really does want to come back,
but she's so stubborn,"
said Brendon, sighing.

That night Gavin phoned Libby again.

He really did want her to come back
to the band.

He missed her.

"Hi Libby, Gavin here."

"Hi Gavin."

"Look Libby, I know you said you
weren't going to come back.
But . . . well, we had a meeting
and we decided that there were
things we could do better.
I've asked Ms Campbell to come and
listen to us play to help us fix things up.
It's good to listen to others and to learn
from them.
What do you think?"

"Yeah, a good idea.
She should know what she's
talking about,"
admitted Libby.

"Well, why don't you join us?"

"No. I'd feel stupid.
I acted really dumb."

"Don't be so stubborn.
We understand why you were upset.
We won't think you're stupid.
We want you back."

"I'll think about it,"
said Libby.

"Look, I want you to come back Libby.
It's not the same without you.
There's no one to tease.
See you at practice on Thursday.
Bye,"
Gavin said, and he quickly put
down the phone.

He could hardly believe he'd
said all that.

But it was true.

He liked her crazy ways and he
missed her.

Would she come?

He could hardly wait until Thursday.

Chapter 2

"Look who's here,"

said Brendon, coming into the sleepout.

"Hi everyone!
I'm back - if you'll have me."

grinned Gavin.

"Great!"
"I'm really pleased you changed
your mind Lib,"
said Estelle.

"I don't know what you said Gavin,
but it worked,"
winked Brendon.

Gavin didn't look at Libby or Brendon
and began sorting music.

"Ms Campbell will be here in half
an hour. Let's get some practice in
before she comes,"
said Gavin hurriedly.

The band had a good run through.

14

When Ms Campbell came they went through the songs again. She gave them lots of help.

They practised each song, trying

out her suggestions.

They repeated some parts lots
of times.

They began to notice the difference
almost immediately.

By the end of the session they
were tired, but satisfied.

"Thanks for all your help Ms Campbell,"
said Brendon.

"Yeah, it was amazing.
You could really hear the difference,"
agreed Estelle.

"It certainly sounded better,"

nodded Libby.
She'd been quiet all night.

"I really enjoyed myself.
It made a change from the orchestra,"
laughed Ms Campbell.
"I'd be happy to come again,
if you would like."

"Would you?"
said Estelle.

"That would be great!"
said Brendon.

"See you next week then,"
called Ms Campbell.

"Thanks, bye!"

they all called.

"You were right Gavin.
Getting an expert in to help was
just what we needed,"
said Estelle.
"A few more practices with
Ms Campbell and we'll be superstars!"

Brendon and Estelle left and
went down the path together.
Libby hung back, fiddling with her
drum set.

"Gavin,"
she said, tentatatively as she went
to leave.
"I - I . . . thanks for the phone call."

"I'm just pleased it worked."
Gavin said.

"You were right.
I was . . .
I did want to come back.
I just . . ."

"Forget it Libby,"
said Gavin.
"I'm glad . . . I mean, we're all just
pleased you're back in the team."

Chapter 3

Martyn was also pleased that Libby
had come back to the band.

He'd got them another booking and
he wanted it to be a success.

With no drummer it would have been
difficult.

His Uncle, a fireman, was in charge
of organising an open day at the
Fire Station.

They were going to give tours
around the Fire Station, put on
displays and let the children look
inside the fire engines.

As well, they wanted some
entertainers there to keep the
crowd happy.

He had asked them to play
throughout the day.

At the Thursday practice Martyn
was surprised by how much
they had improved with
Ms Campbell's help.

"You've really improved since I
heard you last.
This open day will be a good
venue to try out your new sound."

"It sounds fun,"
agreed Libby.

"Can your Dad take the gear on
Sunday, Brendon?"
asked Martyn.

"No problem."

"What time will we need to be
set up by?"
Gavin wanted to know.

They spent the next half hour
making sure that everyone knew
all the details for Sunday.

Sunday was a beautiful day -
ideal for families to come and
enjoy the open day.

The band was set up and ready to
go by 10 am. They were keen to play
and itching to get started.

"No point in beginning until there's a crowd,"
suggested Martyn's Uncle Pete.

"No, we'll give it a bit longer,"
agreed Martyn.

Time ticked away.

Chapter 4

By 10:30 am the people had
begun to arrive.

Uncle Pete signalled that the band
should begin to play.

Brendon called the other three to
him and said,

"Okay!
Now remember what we've
been practising.
Let's not let all that hard work and
Ms Campbell's help go to waste.
Let's give it everything we've got."

"Yes, big brother,"
said Libby saluting.
All her cheek and spark had
returned.

"Good luck,"
whispered Gavin quietly to Libby,
as they moved towards
their places.

"Thanks for that Gavin.
I am feeling a bit nervous,"
replied Libby, flashing him a
sparkling smile.

"You'll be fine,"
he said quickly.
He turned away, blushing.

As they began to play, the people
walking past stopped and listened.

At the end of each song, they
clapped warmly.

By the afternoon the band was really
enjoying themselves.

They sounded good and the large
crowd liked them.

Many had stopped there for a long
time, just to listen.

Everything was going well and things
were going to get even better.

During one of their breaks,
Martyn came bounding up
to them.

As he approached he shouted,
"You've done it!
You've done it!"

"Done what?"
asked Libby.

"You know Joe McKenzie?"

"He's the owner of the UndaRage
Nightclub isn't he? The nightclub
for teenagers?"
replied Brendon.

"Yes, that's right.

He wants us to play there on Friday,"

said Martyn. He was jumping about

and couldn't stop smiling.

"He said if it goes well, he might be
able to give us a regular booking,"

"Wow, a regular booking,"
said Estelle.

"Well done Martyn,"
said Brendon, warmly.

"You've done all the hard work,
not me,"
laughed Martyn.

"That's true, but you've worked
hard too.
You got us the chance to play here,
and now a booking for Friday,"
said Gavin.

"That's right.

I didn't think we needed you as our manager to begin with,"

said Libby.

"But now I see you are just what we needed.

Let's all agree that Martyn's trial period is over."

"I'll second that,"

said Gavin quickly.

"All in favour? Carried,"

finished Libby.

"Thanks Libby.

Thanks everyone.

I'm enjoying the challenge,"

smiled Martyn.

Pete came up to them.

"Time for some more music, I think.
Everyone's asking when New Thyme
is going to play again.
You've really done well today.
The people have stayed longer to
enjoy your music.
The whole day has been a huge
success."

During their final numbers, Estelle
spotted Ms Campbell in the crowd.

She was smiling from ear to ear.

At the end of the last song she gave
them the thumbs up. She moved
through the crowd to the stage they

were playing on.

She patted Brendon on the back.

"That sounded pretty good to me.

I've decided that I'm not such a bad

rock band teacher after all."

"Not bad?

You're the greatest!

We couldn't have done it without you.

Thanks a million.

We've got another booking!

This has been such an awesome day!"

the band enthused to

Ms Campbell.

Chapter 5

New Thyme performed at the
UndaRage Nightclub the
following Friday.
They were a hit.

Joe McKenzie asked them to play
again the next week.

As well as the excitement of playing
again the next week, they had the
thrill of receiving their first pay cheque
- their first paying booking.

TEB

PAY _New Thyme_ DATE _12 Nov 95_

THE SUM OF _Two Hundred dollars_

$ 200.00

UNDERAGE NIGHTCLUB

" 87001 "0423119: 0678 "00

"I think we should bank the money
at first until we build up enough to
buy new gear,"
suggested Martyn.
"Then when we have enough we
can divide it up and get
some each."

"That makes sense to me,"
agreed Estelle.

"Good idea,"
nodded Brendon.

"Yeah, me too.
As long as it doesn't take
too long!"
laughed Libby.

"It'll be good to earn some money
while having fun.
I've been wondering what to do to
save for my education.
Now my problem's solved,"
said Gavin.

"That's right.
Mum and Dad have been on at me to
begin doing that too,"
agreed Estelle.

"It's all worked out really well.
Listening to some good advice, sticking
at it and putting in some hard work,
have really paid off,"
said Brendon.

They all agreed that the band had
been a positive thing for all of them.

They'd learnt and grown a lot.

The future looked bright.